three c......
memories of the ....
coast. Her first book w.......... *....er Pickers*, and
she has since written many other titles, including
Riding the Waves (Commended for the 1991
Carnegie Medal), *Haunted House Blues* and the
Time Spinners trilogy: *Meet Me By the Steelmen*,
Night of the Red Devil and *Scavenger Boy*. "I write
full-time now," she says. "I love it." Theresa
Tomlinson now lives in Sheffield with her architect
husband and her cat, Mewsli.

Books by the same author

The Flither Pickers
Haunted House Blues
Riding the Waves

Time Spinners:

Scavenger Boy
Night of the Red Devil

MEET ME
BY THE
STEELMEN

THERESA TOMLINSON

illustrations by

ANTHONY LEWIS

WALKER BOOKS
AND SUBSIDIARIES
LONDON • BOSTON • SYDNEY

In memory of Jack Louis Casling Simpson

First published 1997 by Walker Books Ltd
87 Vauxhall Walk, London SE11 5HJ

This edition published 2003

2 4 6 8 10 9 7 5 3 1

Text © 1997 Theresa Tomlinson
Illustrations © 1997 Anthony Lewis
Cover illustration © 2003

The right of Theresa Tomlinson to be identified as
author of this work has been asserted by her in accordance
with the Copyright, Designs and Patents Act 1988

This book has been typeset in Plantin

Printed in Great Britain by
Cox & Wyman Ltd, Reading, Berkshire

British Library Cataloguing in Publication Data:
a catalogue record for this book
is available from the British Library

ISBN 0-7445-8988-6

Contents

The Statues

....

They stood head and shoulders above the
crowd of shoppers, three giants cast in
bronze. Three Sheffield steelmen. Our Stevie
had been mad about them, ever since
Meadow Hall shopping centre first opened.
All he wanted to do was stand beside the
huge statues, staring up at them.

"Jenny ... keep your eye on Stevie," said
Mum. "Wait here and don't wander off. It
looks as though there's going to be some
music or a band on."

She nodded to where men in overalls were
putting up a platform on the other side of the
lift. A small crowd was gathering about the
stage.

"OK," I said.

Mum went into the vast supermarket that
sold everything from food to furniture.

I sighed. It was the school holidays and Meadow Hall is a wonderful place to be if you're free to wander and buy and taste and smell. But if you've got a nuisance of a seven-year-old brother to look after, it spoils it all.

"Come on," I said, grabbing his arm. "Let's look at the cake stall. I'll buy you a jammy doughnut or one of those special iced biscuits."

But Stevie shook his head. "No," he said, seriously. "I've got to watch the men."

He's weird, my brother. Other young kids whined around the chocolate stall, their mouths dribbling at the luscious display. Not our Stevie, all he wanted to do was watch the three steelmen.

There was giggling behind me and Sue and Amy from school rushed up. They grabbed me, one on each side.

"Hi, Jenny!"

"We thought it was you. Have you come to see the band? They're supposed to be on in five minutes. They're really loud and they

dance too. Sally's cousin's in it."

I pulled a miserable face and nodded at our Stevie. "I'm supposed to be keeping an eye on him."

"He'll be all right," said Amy. "You can still see him from over there. We want to get to the front of the stage."

I turned and looked at Stevie. He wasn't going to run off anywhere, I could be pretty sure of that. Bending down close, I whispered in his ear. "I'm going to listen to the band. You stay right here. Do you hear? Don't move!"

He didn't answer, but he nodded his head. He never took his eyes from the statues.

We pushed our way through the crowd until we stood at the front of the stage.

"What's going on over there?" I said, nodding at the shop behind the stage. It was full of security guards and even a policeman.

"That's the third policeman I've seen here today," said Sue.

"There's something up," I agreed.

"It must be a break-in!" said Amy. "The shutters are still down … but look at them!"

Then I saw that one of the strong fancy metal shutters that protect the shops at night had a hole in it. It wasn't a big hole, just wide enough to get your hand through.

"But … aren't they made of steel, those shutters?"

"I thought they were," said Amy. "They're certainly tough. I know, I've tried to swing on them!"

"Look at the edges of the hole," said Sue. "It's as if it's been melted."

"But *why* would anyone do that?" I asked. "Why break into a shop that sells Yorkshire puddings? I mean, look … there's a jewellers' next door with diamond rings and necklaces."

We all stared as the police measured the hole in the metal. You could see from their faces that they were as puzzled as we were.

"Perhaps whoever did it was hungry," said Amy.

Then all at once the members of the band were jumping up on to the stage and snatching up their instruments. They weren't famous or anything, but they were good and we all started clapping our hands and dancing along with them. It was exciting, what with the thudding music and the plastic palm trees swaying gently as we all jigged about.

It was so lovely that I completely forgot about Stevie, and I only remembered him again when the band stopped and everyone cheered. "Oh help!" I said. "My brother!"

I pushed my way back through the crowd, but I needn't have worried. Mum wasn't back yet and, of course, Stevie hadn't moved. "Great band," I said. "Could you hear them?"

He nodded but didn't speak, then I saw that his cheeks had gone very white. I felt bad for leaving him.

"Are you all right?" I asked, putting my hand out to touch his shoulder.

"Yes," said Stevie. "I'm all right, but I got a bit scared. *He* looked at me."

He pointed up at the smallest statue; a young lad holding out a rod.

I laughed. "Don't be so silly."

"He moved his head," Stevie insisted. "And he looked right at me. He stuck out his tongue."

A strange shuddery feeling crept up my back. Stevie was so pale and so certain that I looked up at the statue myself.

Even though it was the smallest of the three, it still towered high above us. The bronze face was tinged with green. The boy looked down at the big pot that another man was tipping, the muscles in his face clenched in concentration. Golden bronze veins stood out on his hands. You could see the woven pattern on his apron and the creases in his heavy clogs. The statues were certainly very lifelike, I had to give Stevie that.

"Come on now. Don't be daft," I said, still shivering a bit.

The Steelman's Pot

"Oh good. You're still here," said Mum.
"Sorry I'm late … I got a bit carried away.
Give us a hand will you?"

She certainly had got carried away. She
usually came out of the supermarket all
loaded up, but that day it was ridiculous.
I took the parcel from under her arm and
a heavy carrier bag.

"Come on, Stevie," said Mum.

"I've got to watch the men," he murmured.

"Come *on*, Stevie. We'll go on the
supertram."

Stevie turned his head at last. "Yeah?"

"Yes," said Mum. "You've been a good lad,
waiting so patiently for me."

The supertram slid smoothly into Meadow
Hall terminus, like a sleek silver serpent. As it

stopped, hissing sounds rose from the brakes. Doors swung open and people poured out of its gaping sides.

"Let me go near the window," Stevie insisted.

Once we were settled in our seats the driver's voice came over the loudspeaker: "Mind the doors, please!" Then we were off.

Our supertram snaked away from the shopping centre towards Sheffield, past two huge grey cooling towers and dusty steelworks. I turned around and watched Meadow Hall shrinking in the distance. It looked like a miniature fairytale castle, with its warm red bricks and green glass dome glinting in the sun.

"I love going there," I told Mum.

"Me too," said Stevie.

When we got back to our terrace we saw Ethel out in her front garden, leaning on the gate, with her grey cat Cokey balancing on top of the fence.

"Oh help!" said Mum. "We're late already. We'll never get past Ethel in time for our lunch."

We all liked Ethel. She was a widow and she lived in the house at the bottom of our street. She had a tiny front garden that she kept bright with tubs and pots of flowers. The only thing about Ethel was that she did like to talk. And how she liked to talk. She often stood leaning on her gate looking out for anyone who'd listen. Once she got going you just couldn't stop her.

"Been to Meadow Hall again, I see."

"Yes, Ethel," said Mum, stopping and putting down her bags. "You know, you should come with us some time."

Ethel shook her head. "Not with my bad leg. Couldn't manage it … all that walking."

"They do have wheelchairs there. If you came with us we'd push you round. Wouldn't we, Jenny?"

I didn't reply. I wasn't sure I'd like to do that. I mean, what if Sue and Amy saw me pushing an old woman round Meadow Hall in a wheelchair? Ethel didn't seem to like the idea much either.

"I'd feel a fool," she said. "Got two legs. It's just that they don't work very well."

Stevie climbed up on Ethel's gate, reaching his hand out to Cokey, who purred and rubbed his chin against Stevie's fingers. Suddenly, he pulled his hand away and pointed at Ethel's door.

"Steelman's pot!" he yelled.

"Get down, Stevie," said Mum. "It's very rude to point and shout like that."

Stevie ignored her. He yelled with excitement. "You've got a steelman's pot!"

We all frowned and stared at Ethel's door, then suddenly Ethel laughed. "Bless him! I know what he means. He's quite right!"

She turned around and hobbled up to her doorstep where a round dark pot stood, filled with nasturtiums. It was quite tall, with burnt lumps down one side that looked as though they'd been dribbled there.

"Our Frank's crucible pot," she said. "He brought it home with him from Hadfield's, the day they closed down the steelworks. He had a struggle to bring it. They're pretty heavy, but do you know what he'd got in it? A tiny grey and white kitten."

"Cokey!" Stevie cried.

"That's right. You see, the steelworks were full of cats."

"Oh dear!" said Mum. "What happened to them all when the works closed?"

"Well … the men took home as many of the kittens as they could manage. They were quite tameable, but the older ones were far too fierce. I'm afraid most of them were just left to fend for themselves. There was a woman who spent days clambering about the place trying to rescue them. She's still got a house full of cats. I give her a donation every Christmas. Must cost so much to feed that lot. She finds good homes for as many as she can, but she keeps the rest."

We stared at Cokey with new interest.

Ethel smiled and shook her head. "But fancy your Stevie knowing that was a steelman's pot! He's a clever lad!"

"It's like the one the Meadow Hall statues have," I told her. "That's how he knows."

Ethel nodded and sniffed. "Aye. Hadfield's steelworks closed and they built that great big shopping centre in its place."

Stevie grabbed Ethel's arm. "The steelmen are still there," he whispered.

Ethel looked a bit puzzled. "Are they, love?"

"He means the statues," I told Ethel hurriedly. Even funny old Ethel might think our Stevie was going mad if he started on about the statues pulling faces at him.

"Now I bet you'd like to see those statues, Ethel," said Mum. "We'll be going again a week next Monday, in the morning. It's nice and quiet then. Come with us?"

"Oh … I don't know."

For once she seemed lost for words.

What's Snap?

Later that night Dad brought in the evening paper. "Did you say you'd been to Meadow Hall?" he said. "There's funny goings on there, according to this report. Now listen ... what do you think?

'...a spate of mysterious break-ins at Sheffield's largest shopping centre. Today's attack on a Yorkshire pudding shop was only the latest in a long list of mysterious attempted robberies that are puzzling police and security guards. The would-be thieves appear to have used a blow torch of considerable power in their attempts to rob the small stores. As yet no actual goods appear to have been taken. The police spokesperson said that they were baffled by the thieves' motives. All the stores concerned sold foodstuffs. To date a

sandwich shop, a sausage shop and a pork
pie speciality shop have all been involved,
along with the Yorkshire pudding shop.
There is no sign of breaking or entering.' "

"I saw it," I said. "I saw this funny hole in the iron shutters. We thought it was melted."

Stevie came and looked at the paper carefully. He couldn't read properly yet, but I could see that he was trying hard, spelling out the words.

"It doesn't make sense," said Mum. "Who'd rob Yorkshire pudding shops when there was really valuable stuff around?"

"Yorkshire puddings are grand if you're hungry," said Dad. "Makes me wonder about these poor homeless folk. What a temptation. All that fancy food on display."

"What's snap?" said Stevie. "Is it food?"

He does ask some crazy questions, just when you're least expecting them.

I clicked my fingers in his face. "That's snap!" I told him, and we all laughed.

*   *   *

Later that night I crept up to bed trying not to wake Stevie. I needn't have bothered. He called me into his room.

"Jenny … Jenny. Come here! What's snap really? Tell me!"

I frowned and sat down on his bed. "What do you mean?" I asked.

"The big man," said Stevie, "the one that's got great long scissors in his hand … he spoke to me. He said, 'Where's our snap?'"

"Spoke?" I said. "Spoke and pulled faces?"

I was very puzzled and a little scared. Stevie was really imagining strange things. I just shook my head.

A week went by and then the following Monday morning we heard a sharp knock on our door. It was very early, before we'd even got out of bed. I went sleepily downstairs to answer it, hoping that it meant the postman must have a parcel for us. Stevie had got there before me. He always got out of bed at the crack of dawn and went down to watch

the telly. He opened the door, still wearing his pyjamas. It was not the postman, it was Ethel, leaning on her walking stick and all dressed up in a smart black suit. She clutched a cream leather handbag and wore a soft cream hat with a sparkly brooch pinned on to it. A faint scent of violets drifted in through our door.

I was amazed and couldn't think what to say. Fortunately, Mum came rustling up behind us in her dressing gown.

"Oh, Ethel," she cried. "Is anything wrong?"

"No," said Ethel. "Just decided that I *would* come with you to that place after all."

"That's lovely," said Mum politely. "I'm afraid we're not ready just yet. Tell you what … we'll call in at your house on our way down, shall we?"

"Oh well," said Ethel. "If that suits you. Our Frank had to be down there at six thirty every morning when he worked at Hadfield's."

"Good grief," I said.

"We won't be long," Mum called after her. "See you, Ethel!"

I shut the door and looked at my watch.

"Eight o'clock!" I said with disgust. "She's got me up at eight o'clock and it's school holidays!"

Mum laughed. "Be glad you're not a steelworker like Ethel's Frank was. Oh dear, fancy her struggling up here at this time."

"She looked like the Queen Mother," I said.

"Well she certainly seems keen to go."

"She looked nice," said Stevie. "And she smelled nice too."

Mum made us rush about, getting ready. She telephoned the shopping centre to see if we could have the use of a wheelchair.

"Oh good," I heard her say. "So it'll be there waiting at the supertram stop."

I sighed. I knew that I'd end up pushing the thing. Mum was a mad shopper and Stevie was too small.

"I don't want my friends to see me with an old woman in a wheelchair," I said.

Mum frowned for a moment, then she laughed. "Well you said she looked like the Queen Mother. Get her to wave graciously and your friends might be impressed."

Another One Hooked!

We had to walk slowly for Ethel, but it wasn't far to the supertram stop.

"Never been on the thing," said Ethel looking rather nervous. "Do you pay the driver?"

"No," said Mum. "We get tickets from machines."

Once we were settled in our seats Ethel seemed quite impressed. "So smooth and quiet. Oh yes … this is the way to travel."

"There's the new stadium," said Mum pointing out of the windows, "and the Arena."

Ethel looked about with interest. "Well, I never," she said. "I wouldn't know the place. If only our Frank could see this!"

The supertram sped on, rolling a little from side to side as it went round bends. When we arrived at Meadow Hall, there was a uniformed man waiting with a wheelchair.

"Push you over the bridge, Madam?" he asked.

"Ooh, I don't like this," said Ethel, but she lowered herself into the seat, gripping the arms. Then we were off over the bridge and down the ramps.

Once we reached the shops the man handed the wheelchair over to Mum.

"Oh, my goodness!" said Ethel. "Look at the size of it! Look at the height! Oh, you were quite right. I couldn't have walked. How lovely … street cafés, just like pictures of France. I always wanted to go to France. Let's have a drink and cakes."

"You've got to see the statues," said Stevie.

"Coffee first," said Ethel. It seemed she'd taken charge.

So we sat out in the covered street and had drinks and buns with pink sticky icing that Ethel insisted on paying for.

When we pushed Ethel along the shopping

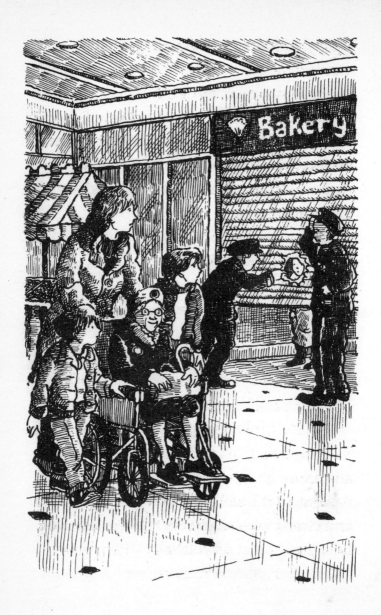

malls, we saw security men examining another melted hole in the iron shutters of a shop. This time it was a bakery.

Food again, I thought. It's always food they're after. Who could be sneaking around Meadow Hall in the night, feeling hungry? And who could manage to melt small holes in strong shutters like that?

We watched clowns juggling in the mall and some dancing teddy bears. We went up and down in the green domed lifts until we were dizzy, and at last we gave in to Stevie and went to look at the statues.

Mum took the opportunity to slip away to the supermarket. "Meet you by the steelmen in half an hour," she said.

So I did push Ethel in her wheelchair along the shopping mall and though I didn't see any of my friends I realized that I wouldn't have cared if I had. Ethel was such good fun and clearly enjoying herself. It was amazing how many other wheelchairs you noticed once you'd got one yourself.

As soon as Ethel saw the statues her eyes went all watery.

"They're wonderful," she said. "Puts me so much in mind of my Frank."

Another one hooked, I thought. Ethel had the same dreamy look in her eyes as Stevie. Those statues seemed really to fascinate people. I was beginning to think that perhaps there *was* something weird about them.

"See the big man with the long scissors?" said Stevie.

Ethel laughed. "They're not scissors," she said. "They're tongs. That big chap … he's the puller-out. He has to be big and strong so that he can haul the heavy pot full of molten steel out of the furnace hole. Now the other chap … he's the teemer, he's the boss! It's his job to carefully pour the white hot melted steel out of the crucible pot into the mould. Look how he clenches his jaw with the strain."

"He hasn't got his scarf in his mouth," said Stevie.

"No," said Ethel.

I frowned and looked. "Did he have his scarf in his mouth before?" I asked.

"Yes, he did," said Stevie.

I tried hard to remember and I didn't contradict our Stevie because I had this awful creepy feeling that he was right. The steelman's scarf hung straight down to the ground and I was sure that he'd had it gripped between his teeth when we'd come before. Ethel was so impressed by the statues that she carried on talking, telling us loads about the ways of steelworkers.

"Now, that smaller one with the rod, he's mopping off the scum that floats to the top, they call it slag. He's the lad, he is. He puts me in mind of my Frank. He looked just like that when I first met him and he worked in the small crucible workshop at Hadfield's."

"Yes," said Stevie. "He's the cheeky one. He sticks his tongue out at people."

"What?" said Ethel.

I hurriedly told her, "They're so lifelike, Stevie thinks they're real."

"I can quite see why," said Ethel. "They really are wonderful in every detail, but … they've got no snap."

"What?" said Stevie. I thought he was going to explode. He grabbed the arm of Ethel's wheelchair and bent close to whisper in her ear. "What *is* snap?"

Ethel laughed. "What's snap? Why it's their dinner, all packed up in a tin. Bread and cheese and nice thick sandwiches. A good slice of fruit cake or a fatty rascal. Maybe a pork pie if they're really lucky. They need plenty of snap, do steelworkers. Without it they'd be *very* hungry."

A Steelman's Picnic

Mum wasn't away for long and we decided to go for our lunch in the big food hall that was decorated to look like an Italian villa. Ethel stared about her, amazed.

"It's a funny café this," she said. "Where's all the waitresses and haven't they got a menu?"

We explained that you had to go up to the stalls and choose what you wanted, then find a table and seats. We decided to have huge Yorkshire puddings with thick onion gravy from the traditional stall. They were filling and delicious, though Stevie couldn't sit still and was soon saying that he was full. I could see that he was bursting with some wild idea. I just hoped that he wouldn't explode there and then.

"Oh, I *am* glad I've come," said Ethel. "It's

so huge and busy and modern. I'm not quite sure I like it, but I'm glad I've seen it all. These Yorkshire puddings are grand, though I can't get used to paper plates and plastic forks."

After we'd finished eating Ethel went rather quiet and worn out looking. Mum said it was time to go home, so we pushed Ethel to the supertram station and handed the wheelchair back to the porter.

"I've had a wonderful day," she told him.

We dropped Ethel off at her house, exhausted but quite talkative again. Cokey jumped up on the gate to meet her. Ethel wagged her finger as the cat purred and rubbed against her hand.

"Oh, Cokey … if you could see your old steelworks now," she said.

That night when I went up to bed I looked in on Stevie again. Just as I'd suspected, he was wide awake and waiting for me.

"Jenny, Jenny," he said. "You saw it didn't you?"

I knew what he meant. "The teemer's scarf?"

He nodded. "They walk about," he whispered. "They go looking for their snap. They do it at night when all the shops are closed."

It was a crazy, terrifying thought, but somehow I began to think that he might be right. I couldn't forget all those security guards puzzling over the strange melted holes in the iron shutters.

"Do you think it's *them* making the holes in the shutters?"

"'Course they are," said Stevie with certainty. "They're steelmen aren't they … they can melt anything."

I sat there on his bed in silence, thinking hard. "Nobody would believe it," I said at last. "Mum and Dad would think we were crazy. The police would think we were messing them about! What can we do?"

"Give them their snap!" Stevie answered. "Give them their dinner!"

"It's not as simple as that," I said. "How can we give them their snap?"

He shrugged his shoulders. "It would have to be the right kind of snap," he said. "Proper steelmen's food."

An idea popped into my head then. Perhaps there was a way. There was certainly someone who knew how to make a steelman's dinner.

"I wonder if we could get Ethel to help," I said. "She'd know how to make just the right kind of snap."

"Yes, yes. That's it!"

We both grinned at each other.

With a great sigh Stevie settled down and pulled up the sheets. "Now I *can* go to sleep," he said.

The following Sunday we went round to see Ethel, just me and Stevie. I felt a bit nervous because we'd never gone there by ourselves before and somehow it seemed a bit of a cheek to ask her to give us food, but Stevie was determined.

"Ethel, Ethel," he said as soon as she opened the door. "We want to have a steelman's picnic. Will you help us make the snap?"

Ethel laughed at his eagerness.

"What is it he wants, Jenny?"

"Stevie's got this idea!" I explained. "He wants to have a picnic near the statues at Meadow Hall, and he wants to eat the kind of food that the steelmen would have eaten."

"It's got to be right," said Stevie, his face all worried. "It's got to be proper steelmen's food."

"Goodness gracious!" Ethel's face lit up. "Come inside the pair of you. You've come to the right place."

Ethel's kitchen was sparkling clean and neat. Cokey kept rubbing round our ankles, purring wildly ... he seemed pleased with his visitors.

"Now," said Ethel. "I'm going to show you something that I treasure. You can borrow it, so long as you keep it safe and bring it back."

Ethel opened a cupboard and brought out a rather battered looking old tin with a hinged lid. I could see that it had once been fancy, but the patterns and pictures on it were faded. You could just see the shape of a woman's head on the side of it.

"My Frank's snap tin," she told us.

Oven Bottom Cakes

Stevie was delighted when he saw the old tin. He jumped up and down. "Yes! Yes! That's just what we need!"

"That's Queen Mary," Ethel pointed to the picture. "Queen Elizabeth's grandmother, she was. And somewhere down here…" Ethel went rooting around in the cupboard again. "Ah, here we are!"

She brought out an old stone-coloured bottle with a cork in the top.

"What goes in there?" Stevie demanded.

"Home-made lemon barley water," said Ethel. "You're in luck. I made some just last week."

The cork crumbled in her hand. "Oh dear! I'll have to find a new one. And you'll have to give that bottle a good clean out first. Now then … you'd both better roll up your sleeves and wash your hands. You've work to do."

Ethel sat at her kitchen table and gave us our orders. We looked in her cupboards and found flour, sugar, currants, sultanas, dried orange peel and butter.

"Home-made bread," said Ethel. "That's the most important thing in the snap tin. We'll make oven bottom cakes too, with the bits of dough left over … my Frank loved those. We didn't waste a thing in those days, we didn't even waste the cooking space at the bottom of the oven. Now, I think I've just enough fresh yeast left. We'll start by creaming it; we want sugar and warm water. Right, Jenny … come on. You can knead the dough."

It wasn't long before Ethel's kitchen was hot and steamy with delicious, mouth-watering smells. We pummelled the dough and left it to rise, then thumped it and kneaded it again, and shaped three round flat bread cakes. We rubbed fat into flour and mixed in dried fruit, then used a round cutter

to make scones. Cokey kept getting in the way. He ended up covered in flour.

We had to work hard. Ethel wouldn't have any slacking, but she let us eat fresh-made scones washed down with her delicious lemon barley water, while we waited for the bread to cool. Then Ethel opened another cupboard and brought out a small tub.

"Potted meat," she said. "Frank's favourite, this used to be. Home-made potted meat then, of course."

She cut thick chunky slices of our home-made bread, and spread them with butter and lashings of potted meat. Then she got another small pot from her fridge.

"Good beef dripping!" she said. "Another thing Frank loved."

She cut open the three oven bottom cakes and filled them with dripping. Then she brought out some cheese and a pork pie and set out three hard-boiled eggs.

"One each for you two and one for your Mum."

Stevie and I grinned at each other. I winked. That would be just right for the three steelmen.

"Now," said Ethel. "Just one more thing."

She looked in her cupboard and brought out a rather worn but snowy white napkin, embroidered with an F in the corner. She used the napkin to line the snap tin and soon a great chunky, delicious picnic was packed inside with a knife that said *Made in Sheffield*. The stone-coloured bottle was filled with lemon barley water.

"Well," said Ethel. "That's it. You won't find a better steelman's picnic than that. You've worn me out again, but I must say I've enjoyed it. It's taken me back."

"Taken you back where?" asked Stevie.

Ethel laughed. "It's made me remember how I used to bake every other day."

"Phew!" I said. "Making Frank's snap must have been hard work."

"Yes, it was," she said. "Then there was stew and dumplings to cook for his supper."

We thanked Ethel and carried our tin and bottle up the road.

"It might be better if Mum doesn't know what we're up to," I said.

Stevie nodded. He really understands a lot, for a little kid.

"I'll run straight upstairs with the stuff," I told him. "And hide it in my duffle bag. Then I'll carry it to Meadow Hall tomorrow."

"Okay," said Stevie. Then he sighed. "I wish *we* had a fluffy grey and white cat like Cokey."

Heat and Dirt

We were both quiet as we sped along in the supertram early on Monday morning. My bag was really heavy and dug into my shoulder, but I didn't complain about it.

As soon as we arrived at Meadow Hall we left Mum, saying, "Meet you by the steelmen in an hour."

I think she was a bit surprised. "You'll keep your eye on Stevie?" she said.

I promised that I would.

We almost ran up the shopping mall. Then, as we turned the corner by the food hall, we saw security guards again.

"It's getting worse," I heard one of them say. "Holes all over these shutters."

It was a fudge and chocolate shop.

"It'll be all right soon," said Stevie. "We've got what they really want."

But as we got closer to the statues, I slowed down.

"Crazy ... I must be crazy," I muttered. "Talking statues!"

For two pins I'd have turned around and gone back to Mum, but Stevie went hurtling on ahead of me. Then, when he reached the steelmen, he came back and snatched the bag from my shoulder.

He was wild with excitement and I couldn't do anything to stop him. His hands were shaking as he pulled out the faded tin and bottle. He stood beside the tall steelman who Ethel called the puller-out.

"We've brought you your snap!" he shouted.

For a few moments we stood there intently watching the statues' green bronze faces. I don't know what we thought would happen.

Suddenly I giggled and looked round, feeling stupid. The girl at the chocolate stall must have thought we were mad. An old man with a big shopping bag wandered round the back of the statues.

"I think we'd better just eat the picnic ourselves," I said.

But Stevie shook his head and pointed to the teemer. "Look at his scarf," he whispered.

I saw then that the teemer gripped his scarf in his mouth once again. There really was something very strange going on. Stevie pushed the bottle at me and tucked the snap tin under his arm, then he put out his hand and touched the bronze apron that the puller-out wore. Very slowly something *did* start to happen.

I noticed faint sounds of clanging, as though somebody further down the mall had dropped something metal and heavy. The sound came again and this time it was louder and then a high whining grating noise followed. It stopped and started ... stopped and started.

"Can you hear it?" Stevie looked at me, his eyes wide.

I nodded. Then beads of sweat prickled my forehead. The air around us grew warmer.

"Can you smell it?" Stevie demanded.

And again I nodded. My nose was twitching with thick metallic dust and the smell of smoke and burning. I stared around wildly, but the sweet stall girl was calmly filling little bags of sweeties. The old man bent to read the small plaque that stood beside the statues.

I felt scared and put my arm around Stevie's shoulders. As soon as I touched him the shops and lifts and gleaming glossy tiles of Meadow Hall seemed to fade, and we were in a different, noisy, shadowy place that was stifling hot.

"Look at the pot!" whispered Stevie.

Gleaming white-golden molten steel poured from the teemer's crucible pot, while sparks floated upwards, vanishing into the darkness above our heads. The steelmen's faces were white in the glare of the liquid steel and the veins in their hands stood out purple against the red of their skin. They didn't tower above us any more. They weren't any bigger than my dad, but I was so scared I couldn't speak or move.

Stevie wasn't scared. "Wow!" he whispered.

Then all at once the pot was poured and the teemer stood the crucible upright on the ground. He sighed with relief and straightened his back. "That's done," he said in a deep voice. "I'm starving hungry. Time for our snap! Where's our snap?"

"We've brought it for you," Stevie yelled.

"At last!" said the puller-out. "They've brought us our snap!"

The young lad stood back and stuck his tongue out at us. I saw that he had a pink rosebud tucked into the top buttonhole on his shirt.

Stevie laughed. "Cheeky!" he said and stuck his tongue out too.

"Don't mess with him," said the puller-out. "He's a good lad … he's brought our snap!"

"He's a grand lad," the teemer's voice rumbled. He swooped down on our Stevie, who still clutched the snap tin, and lifted him,

hoisting him easily up on to his shoulder. "Come on then, Frank," he said to the lad with the rod. "We'll eat it in the yard."

I had to let go of Stevie's hand as he was hitched up on to the teemer's shoulder and, as I let go, the noise and heat started to fade. Suddenly I was back among the shops and brightness of Meadow Hall, holding the old bottle. The statues stood solidly in front of me, but Stevie wasn't there.

It was a terrible moment. I felt sick and sweaty and *so* scared. Where was Stevie? I was back in Meadow Hall, but he wasn't. What would I tell Mum? I looked frantically around for help, but the shop assistants ignored me and got on with their work. The old man was still reading the plaque.

I couldn't leave Stevie like that! I didn't know what might happen to him! I'd promised Mum that I'd look after him and now I didn't even know exactly where he was!

Just Like Cokey

....

"I've lost my brother!" I shouted.

The old man looked up at me. "Don't worry, love," he said kindly. "The shop assistants will find him for you. Go and ask the young lady."

He nodded towards the girl on the sweet stall.

I couldn't think what else to do so I ran over to her and shouted again. "I've lost my little brother!"

At once she was all kindness and concern. "Don't worry," she said, "I can phone through to the office. They'll announce it over the loud speaker. What's his name and how old is he?"

My hands were shaking and my voice kept going all husky.

"Stevie," I said.

"Stevie what, dear?"

"He's Stevie Thompson and he's seven years old."

It was amazing how quickly it happened. Before I knew it, the calm voice of the lady announcer was saying, "Will seven-year-old Stevie Thompson please meet his sister by the steelmen statues? I repeat, will seven-year-old Stevie Thompson please go immediately to the statues, where his sister is waiting for him!"

It was brilliant the way they did it, but I was still worried to bits as I went back to the statues. I knew deep down that however helpful the shop people were, they couldn't get Stevie back for me. I could only think of one thing to do: I lurched forwards and grabbed the long apron of the puller-out.

At once the hard bronze turned scratchy and warm in my hands. I was back in all the heat and dirt, clinging to the steelman's apron ... but best of all, there was Stevie perched up on the teemer's shoulder, laughing down at me.

"Where did you go?" he asked. "*You've* got the drink."

There was no time to answer, for all three steelmen set off at a good pace, their heavy clogs clomping as they walked. I followed fast, making sure I kept tight hold of the puller-out's rough apron. They went out of their small workshop with the furnace holes in the floor, and clattered down stone steps into a huge, gigantic shed, filled with the echoing sounds of work. Giant furnace tubs shot sprays of gleaming sparks into the air above, while others tipped, so that golden-white streams of molten steel poured out into long thin moulds.

"Like bonfire night," Stevie yelled.

Sweat poured from my skin. Men with fine metal mesh over their faces shouted and hammered. They looked like olden days knights dressed in chain mail. The sounds were deafening, sparks flashed and glittered, flames roared and flared all about us.

"Fireworks!" Stevie cried.

Then at last we were stepping outside into cool fresh air.

The teemer swung Stevie down to the ground. I put down the bottle and grabbed tight hold of his sleeve. With my other hand I still clung to the puller-out's apron. I was scared of losing touch and slipping back to the shops again … he didn't seem to mind. The men settled themselves on a pile of iron girders and Stevie presented them with the snap box.

They shouted with joy and cheered loudly as they found the pork pie and the dripping bread cakes.

"Now, this is what I call proper snap!" the teemer said.

The young one pulled open a chunky potted meat sandwich and sniffed the butter and meat paste.

"My favourite!" he said. "Just what I like! How did you know?"

"Are you Frank?" Stevie asked.

"That's my name," he said and he tucked into the sandwich, chewing hard. His white teeth gleamed against the dusty grey dirt on his cheeks.

"Do you know somebody called Ethel?"

Frank frowned at first, then a grin spread over his face. "Ethel? Ethel? Oh yes ... of course I do! Cheeky little lass with dark hair. Met her at the dance last Saturday. Oh, she can dance, can that Ethel! Do you know her too?"

We both grinned. "Yes, we know Ethel."

Stevie pulled at my sleeve. "Do you know where we are?" he whispered.

"I think we're at Hadfield's works," I told him. "I don't know how we've managed it, but it seems to be long ago!"

Stevie didn't care, he was so happy. "Perhaps we've been taken back ... like Ethel said. I told you they could move ... didn't I?"

I nodded. It was all crazy but he'd been right.

Suddenly Stevie nudged my arm again and

pointed carefully at the teemer's feet. The man cheerfully munched a good slice of pork pie. As he ate, tiny pieces dropped down to the ground then, fast as could be, a furry grey and white head with whiskers whipped out from between the stack of girders. A pink tongue flashed and the meat was gone.

"A cat … was it a cat?"

"That's Bessie Bessemer," the teemer laughed. "Best mouser in the works." He picked a good sized bit of pork out of his pie and dropped it on to the ground. There was the flash of a tail, a wild growl, and we saw the cat again.

"Yes!" said Stevie. "Grey and white … just like Cokey."

Stevie held out his fingers towards the cat.

"Watch her!" said Frank. "I think she's got kittens hidden under there. She's far too fierce to touch."

Can We Get Home?

Stevie sighed. "I love it here," he said.

"Yes," I said. "But how can we get home?"

His excited laugh told me that he didn't really care.

"But what about Mum?" I said. "She'll be so worried! If we let go I think we'll go back to the shopping centre." I showed him how tightly I held on to the puller-out. "I daren't let go out here in the yard. Who knows where we'd end up? I think we've got to get back to where the crucible pots are poured."

Stevie nodded solemnly. He seemed to understand what I meant. I might have started to get a bit worried that we'd sit out there in the old steelworks yard for ever, but the men had eaten all the food and the teemer stood up.

"Time to get that other pot out," he said.

Frank picked up Ethel's old snap tin and bottle and handed them back to Stevie. "Thank you for our snap," he said. "That was a grand feed. It will fill me up for ever."

Stevie bent down close to the pile of girders. "Goodbye, Bessie Bessemer," he said. "Look after your kittens."

Then the men were off again, striding back through the great shed with the sprays of flaring sparks and the huge tipping machines. I had to run to keep hold of the puller-out's scratchy apron, and I clung to Stevie's sleeve with my other hand.

Back in their workshop the men set about lifting another crucible pot out of a glowing hole in the floor. The puller-out hauled it up with his straight tongs, and I was quite close. The heat made me sweat terribly.

Then the teemer clamped his strong rounded tongs about the middle of the pot. He strained and groaned and bent his knee, and steadily a stream of white-golden melted steel poured out into the mould.

Frank bent to skim the slag from the top with his rod. I knew that was the right moment.

"Now," I whispered to Stevie. I let go of the apron and the men and the bright pouring steel shimmered. The heat faded and suddenly there were bright lights all around us and gentle music playing. We were back in Meadow Hall and Stevie still held Ethel's tin and bottle.

The old man looked across at us. "Oh, there you are," he said. "You see ... you needn't have worried. I told you they'd find your brother for you."

He didn't seem to have moved, or even noticed that we'd been away. The statues stood huge and solid before us and I suddenly felt very tired. Stevie shook Ethel's tin and it rattled. "It feels light," he said. "I think the food has really gone."

He struggled to open the lid and there inside was the napkin and knife and a few crumbs ... and something else. Stevie took out a bright golden brown coin with a man's head on it.

"Good heavens!" said the old man. "I haven't seen one of those for years."

"It's a king," said Stevie. "We usually have a queen on our money."

"George the Fifth penny," the man told him. "Mint condition. You want to take that to the little coin dealers, in the alleyway. Could be worth quite a bit, that."

"You mean they might buy it off us?" I asked.

"Certain they will."

"Oh there you are, you two!" Mum came towards us, a worried look on her face. "I heard over the loudspeakers that Stevie was lost."

"It was just for a moment," I told her. "Look … we've found an old penny. It might be valuable. We're going to ask at the coin dealer's shop."

We raced off to the small row of shops in the alleyway. The coin dealer looked surprised and pleased when we held up the gleaming coin.

"Absolutely mint condition," he said. "I could give you five pounds for that."

"Yes, please," said Stevie.

"We could give Ethel the five pounds," I whispered.

"Yes, we will," Stevie agreed. "Can we have some dinner now, Mum? I'm starving."

So we went into the food hall and had chip butties and lemonade.

We called in at Ethel's house on our way home. Mum went ahead with the shopping. Cokey jumped down from the gate to meet us and Ethel opened the door.

Stevie pushed the snap tin into her hands. "Open the tin," he said. "There's something in it for you."

"Something for me?" Ethel smiled. "Was the picnic good?"

"It was brilliant," I told her. "Open the tin."

When she did pull off the lid we were just as surprised as she was, for there inside with the napkin and the knife and the five pound note was a pink rosebud. It was all dried up and crisp, but it was still beautiful.

"Oh goodness!" Ethel cried. And she picked up the rose and sniffed at it. "It still smells," she said. "Just faintly."

"The five pound note is for you," said Stevie.

"Oh no," said Ethel.

"Do take it," I said. "We found a George the Fifth penny … in mint condition. The coin dealer gave us five pounds for it. You made us a lovely picnic and it must have cost a lot."

But Ethel shook her head. "The rose is all I want."

"What shall we do with it then?" said Stevie.

Ethel thought for a moment, then she said, "I know a Mrs Jones who would find it very useful!"

Bessie Bessemer's Children

···

That afternoon we set out from our house
with Mum. We'd got an address written on a
scrap of paper in Ethel's neat handwriting.

"Now, let me see," said Mum. "I don't
think it's too far. Oh yes, up this road, second
turning on the left. Are you sure you want to
do this?"

"Oh yes," we insisted.

We found the street. It had old houses and
big gardens.

"Number ten," I said checking Ethel's
note.

"*That* must be it," said Stevie running
ahead and pointing.

At the very end of the row was a house the
same size as the others, but rather worn and
in need of decoration. It had a good-sized
garden with an apple tree and grass. The bark

of the tree was scratched and rough and in its branches sat seven cats, all shapes and sizes.

"This has *got* to be it," Stevie shouted.

"I think he's right," said Mum.

Three more cats, all grey and white, sat on the wall at the front. As Stevie approached, snapping his fingers at them, they rushed towards him as though they thought he'd brought them food. Two more jumped down from the tree.

We opened the gate and walked up to the peeling front door, followed by a trail of cats.

A tall woman with grey hair opened the door just a little way, in answer to our knock. "Yes?" she spoke sharply.

"Are you Mrs Jones? Are you the woman who rescued the steelworks cats?" Stevie asked.

The door opened a little wider and we saw that the woman looked worried. "Yes, I am."

Stevie waved the five pound note at her. "This is for you," he said. "You can buy the cats some food."

The door opened wider then and Mrs

Jones smiled. "Do come in," she said. "I thought it was more complaints."

We stepped inside and went into a cosy room, with scuffed paintwork and furniture. A faint catty smell hung in the air. Five more cats curled up by the fire on cushions. They got up, purring like mad as Stevie and I set about giving them all a stroke.

"Oh dear," said Mum. "Have you been getting a lot of complaints?"

Mrs Jones nodded. "The neighbours don't like it!" she said. "I'm afraid it's getting very difficult to keep going. It does take a lot of money to feed them. I'm grateful for your five pounds."

"It's not much," said Mum. "Not when you've got all these."

"Oh, Mum," said Stevie. "Couldn't we have some of them? Take them home?"

Mum sighed and shook her head.

"I'm afraid we have no kittens," said Mrs Jones. "We had them neutered you see … it was the only way. These are all old cats now, and I'm getting old too." She laughed and suddenly looked quite jolly.

"Are they all the children of the steelworks cats?" I asked.

"Yes," said Mrs Jones. "Though some of these are the grandchildren or even great-grandchildren."

"Oh, Mum?" said Stevie.

"I think we've got enough to do just looking after you two," Mum said firmly.

Mrs Jones looked a little hesitant, then she spoke. "If you like cats… if you really love cats … would you like a little job? I could really do with somebody at the weekends to help me feed and groom and clean up."

"Oh yes," said Stevie. "Can I do that?"

"It'll be hard work," Mrs Jones insisted.

"We'll both come," I said.

Mum smiled. "If you two work hard for six weeks, helping Mrs Jones, then you can choose one cat to bring home with you. How about that?"

"Yes!" Stevie cheered.

Two weeks passed and we went shopping to Meadow Hall again. There were no more damaged shutters or melted holes.

Stevie went to stand by the statues for a minute or two. He touched the puller-out's apron, but it stayed cold and hard.

He shook his head. "They won't move again," he said.

"No," I agreed. "They got what they wanted. Come on … we've got to get some cat food for Mrs Jones."

"Just a minute," he said.

Stevie walked round to the statue of the young lad with the rod. "Don't you worry, Frank," he whispered. "We're looking after the steelworks cats and we're looking after Ethel too."

SCAVENGER BOY

Theresa Tomlinson

Michael buys a wooden bobbin the day he moves to his new home in Cromford village. Old and cracked, with the letters FL carved into it, the bobbin rolls backwards and forwards, turning in his hand as if it has a life of its own. Then, one snowy day, Michael finds himself turning too ... and all of a sudden he's back two hundred years among the weavers and their children – the scavengers – working in a local cotton mill.

NIGHT OF THE RED DEVIL

Theresa Tomlinson

In the middle of a family holiday in Whitby, Sam makes two amazing discoveries: a hidden room behind a door in his wardrobe and a lump of jet on the beach. Together they draw him into an incredible adventure – one that takes him back in time over a hundred years, to the world and the work of the mysterious red devils. Will Sam change the course of history?